Marching through the snow after the big game

The English Roses

A Perfect Pair

CALLAWAY ARTS & ENTERTAINMENT

19 FULTON STREET, FIFTH FLOOR, NEW YORK, NEW YORK 10038

PUFFIN BOOKS

Published by the Penguin Group
Penguin Young Readers Group, 345 Hudson Street, New York, New York 10014, U.S.A.
Penguin Group (Canada), 90 Eglinton Avenue East, Suite 700, Toronto, Ontario,
Canada M4P 2Y3 (a division of Pearson Penguin Canada Inc.)

Penguin Books Ltd., Registered Offices: 80 Strand, London WC2R 0RL, England

First published in the United States of America by Callaway Arts & Entertainment and Puffin Books, 2009

1   3   5   7   9   10   8   6   4   2

First Edition

Produced by Callaway Arts & Entertainment
Nicholas Callaway, President and Publisher
Cathy Ferrara, Managing Editor and Production Director
Toshiya Masuda, Art Director • Nelson Gómez, Director of Digital Technology
Joya Rajadhyaksha, Editor • Amy Cloud, Editor
Ivan Wong, Jr. and José Rodríguez, Production
Jennifer Caffrey, Publishing Assistant

Special thanks to Doug Whiteman and Mariann Donato.

Library of Congress Cataloging-in-Publication Data is available.

Puffin Books ISBN 978-0-14-241125-4

Printed in the United States of America

www.madonna.com   www.callaway.com   www.penguin.com/youngreaders

All of Madonna's proceeds from this book will be donated to
Raising Malawi (www.raisingmalawi.org), an orphan-care initiative.

The English Roses

by Madonna

With Erica Ottenberg

A Perfect Pair

PUFFIN
CALLAWAY

New York
2009

illustrated by Jeffrey Fulvimari

Book 8

Contents

CHAPTER I

Monday, Monday

You absolutely, positively, without a doubt must know the English Roses by now. First of all, you could not possibly have gotten this far in life without meeting the five best friends: Binah Rossi, Charlotte Ginsberg, Amy Brook, Grace Harrison, and Nicole Rissman. And secondly, if you didn't know (and, of course, love!) the

English Roses by now, you'd never have picked up this book in the first place!

Ah, Monday. It can be a rather . . . difficult day. After all, you've just spent a wonderful weekend shopping, or watching movies, or reading, or catching up with friends. And then Monday rears its ugly head. And you have to set an alarm, wake up early, and go to school!

But as much as Mondays might bother some, for others they're not all that bad. And for one person in particular, they could actually be quite enjoyable.

"Ugggh!" Charlotte moaned on one very cold, rather gray, extremely long-seeming Monday afternoon. "Isn't this day over yet?" (*Psst!* Charlotte is not the one person in particular who enjoys Mondays!)

"Seriously," Grace replied. "I can't wait to get to the game!" February is not typically football season ("football," what Americans typically refer to as "soccer"). But at Hampstead School, every season was football season. The football field actually had a retractable roof, so when it got too cold to play outside, a glass ceiling enclosed the field and protected the players (and fans) from the elements.

"We'd better win," Grace continued. "We can't let Yorkshire beat us." Yorkshire School was Hampstead's biggest rival. And not just in football; they competed intensely in every sport and every subject.

"I know," said Amy, shaking her head so her red curls bounced around her rosy cheeks. "And can you believe we're having our Valentine's Day Dance with Yorkshire this year? What were people thinking?"

"They can't all be so bad . . ." offered Binah diplomatically. "Right?"

"Well, I guess there are bound to be some new boys there, at least," Amy replied.

Though Amy had a crush on dreamy Ryan Hudson, the chance to meet new (hopefully cute!)

boys was definitely a silver lining to the Yorkshire cloud, in her opinion!

"Ladies, please. This is Science class, not Social Hour." Their teacher, Mrs. Moss, eyed them from the front of the room. The English Roses quieted down. It's just that sometimes it's so hard not to talk when you're not supposed to be talking when there's just so much to talk about!

"Can anyone give me the answer to number four? Anyone?" Mrs. Moss glanced around the room. One single hand was raised.

Mrs. Moss sighed. "Anyone besides Nicole."

Nicole kept her hand raised, smiling brightly. While her friends were more taken with talk of

boys or football (or boys playing football), nothing could distract Nicole from class. It was the first day of a whole week of learning ahead! And what could be better than that?

"Jamie. How about you." All heads turned to the back of the room, where football star Jamie Somers and his seatmate were immersed in a rousing game of tic-tac-toe on the back of Jamie's Science notebook. His sandy blond hair was swept across his forehead, a few strands falling in front of his aqua blue eyes. He looked up. Mrs. Moss continued:

"The answer, Jamie, to question number four. If you please."

Jamie tilted back in his seat. "Four, four . . ." he mused to himself, clearly at a loss for a reasonable answer. "Un-four-tunately, I seem to have four-gotten, Mrs. Moss!" he exclaimed. The class giggled.

Nicole stretched her hand a bit higher, silently appealing to Mrs. Moss with her eyes. She didn't know why everyone thought Jamie Somers was so great. There's a time for joking around, and there's a time for learning. And I'm sure you can guess what time Nicole currently thought it was.

"All right. Nicole." Mrs. Moss finally gave in.

"The answer is 'photosynthesis,'" Nicole proclaimed confidently. She didn't even need Mrs. Moss's nod to tell her she was right.

"Class, the Science Fair is approaching. I'm sure you're all eagerly awaiting the big day on Friday, February fourteenth." The class was silent, but Nicole felt like cheering. The Science Fair was her favorite day of the year. Hampstead competed against—you guessed it—Yorkshire in an annual epic battle. And for Nicole it was personal. She and her archrival, Yorkshire student Jude Matthews, were always neck and neck for first place. He'd beaten her by a hair last year, and this year she was determined not to let it happen again.

"This year, things will be slightly different," Mrs. Moss proclaimed. "You will all be working in pairs. You must pick a partner—and a project—by the start of class tomorrow."

Riiiing! The bell signaled the end of the day. And the English Roses were among the first out the door.

A Tale of 2 Jerseys...

OUR SIDE   THEM

FIRST PLACE

CHAPTER 2

Albert Einstein, Where Are You?

Quilted down jackets with furry hoods, cashmere scarves in radiant colors, knit hats and fluffy mittens were piled on the floor beside them as the girls readied themselves for the game. "Science Fair partners! That's the best news we've gotten from Mrs. Moss

in a long time," Amy said. The girls liked their teacher, but she didn't quite compare to their favorite—Miss Fluffernutter—from last year.

"I know—a partner means half the work!" Charlotte exclaimed. "Remember last year when I almost didn't finish in time? Winston had to bring me double espressos every hour so I could

"Your double espresso, Miss Charlotte..."

stay up all night and get it done." She shuddered at the memory. "My hair looked just awful the next day!" Winston was the Ginsberg family butler. Charlotte's family was extremely wealthy; they also had a cook and even a driver.

"Yeah, well, I'm the worst at Science no matter what. I could have Albert Einstein as a partner; it wouldn't do much good," Amy said.

"That's not true, Aim," Binah reassured her friend. "Anyone would be lucky to be paired with you."

Now, even though Science is the subject at hand, here's a bit of mathematics for you. Five English Roses working in pairs of two. That leaves . . . one odd man out! Or one odd girl, as the case may be. But before you worry yourself into a tizzy, one English Rose has a solution. Can you guess who? Here's a hint: She loves Mondays!

"Well, I'm going to go solo," Nicole said. "I already have my whole project all planned out. Besides, the will to beat Jude Matthews is all the help I need!"

And so it was decided. As they walked out into the icy February air, across the grounds of Hampstead and into the glass-domed football field, the four remaining Roses teamed up. Amy and Charlotte on one hand, Binah and Grace on the other, and Nicole finishing out the five-some, going it alone.

CHAPTER 3

Hampstead vs. Yorkshire

"Let's go, Hampstead!" *Clap clap clap!* "Let's go, Hampstead!" *Clap clap clap!* The stadium was filled to capacity with cheering fans: Hampstead on one side, Yorkshire on the other. Cheerleaders defied gravity with aerial kicks and back handsprings, pom-poms waving. Binah, Amy, Charlotte, Nicole, and Grace sat smack in the middle of the crowd in the bleachers.

"Now, see this?" Charlotte asked, pointing to a headline on the front page of the school newspaper, the *Hampstead Hornblower*. In boldface type, it read: VALENTINE'S VIEW: HAMPSTEAD AND YORKSHIRE DANCE TOGETHER, FEBRUARY 14TH. "That is what we should be focusing on. Not the Science Fair!" Catching a sidelong glance from Nicole, she quickly rephrased. "Sorry, Nikki. I know the Science Fair is your thing. And it is important!" Nicole smiled, placated. Charlotte held up the paper. "But the Valentine's Dance is on the same night! And we need to look hot. I just want to make sure

our priorities are in order."

"Agreed," Amy nodded. "I think we all need new outfits. We've got to make a good showing and impress Yorkshire. Show them how Hampstead girls do things!"

"Whoo!" A huge cheer surged through the stadium as down on the field, Jamie Somers shot the ball right past the Yorkshire goalkeeper, putting Hampstead just one goal behind Yorkshire with ten minutes left to play. The Hampstead crowd went wild.

"Wow." Amy sighed. "Isn't Jamie just the most?"

"The most what?" Nicole asked. "The most annoying? The most distracting?"

"But he is cute," Binah offered. The Roses giggled. "What?" Binah blushed. "He is!"

"For sure," Charlotte agreed.

"And he's amazing on that field," Grace added. "Our team would be lost without him." Helping make her point, the boys of the Hampstead football team clapped Jamie on the back enthusiastically as they cheered his goal.

"I just don't see what the big deal is," Nicole countered. "Being good at football isn't all there is to life." She held up one finger. "He's a slacker." And another: "A joker." A third, fourth, and fifth: "Irresponsible, disrespectful, and not very bright." She waggled her fingers in the air. "Cute can only get you so far."

"And that's time!" The ref blew his whistle and yelled from the field below. "Yorkshire with the win!" The Hampstead side of the stadium fell quiet as the Yorkshire fans erupted in cheers. Dejected, the English Roses followed the crowd of game goers as they filed out of the stadium.

"Well, that stinks," said Grace glumly.

"I know," Amy said, sighing. "Yorkshire will never let us live this down."

"We did score, at least," Binah said, trying to sound sunny. "At least it wasn't—"

"Hello, Nicole." A voice behind them interrupted Binah's pep talk. The English Roses all turned around.

"Hello, Jude," Nicole replied. She certainly didn't sound very happy to see him!

"Sorry about the game," Jude said, looking at her through black-plastic-framed glasses that matched his black hair, black long-sleeved T-shirt, black plastic digital watch, and black sneakers. The only item of color Jude wore was a pair of distressed denim blue jeans. He held out a hand for Nicole to shake. "No hard feelings?"

Nicole's eyes narrowed. Reluctantly, she accepted his hand and shook it.

"But it's probably for the best," Jude said, cocking his head and smiling. "I mean, you should get used to losing before the Science Fair."

Nicole squeezed his hand a bit harder than was necessary as she gave it one final shake. "Oh, don't worry," she retorted. "You'll have losing down to a science soon enough!" She could feel her friends smile with pride behind her. It's always easier to come up with smart one-liners when you've got four best friends backing you up!

"Well. Good luck with your project, anyway," Jude said. His brown eyes softened. "You're definitely the one to beat."

"You got that right!" Grace called after him as he left to rejoin his friends on the Yorkshire side of the field.

Malt shoppe memories

CHAPTER 4

Winning Isn't the Only Thing

"Nicole? Sweetie, how was the game?"

"Hmm?" Nicole barely looked up from her work. She hadn't even heard her mother knocking at her bedroom door. "Good. It was good."

Mrs. Rissman eased the door open a crack and peeked into the room. Nicole was sitting at her desk, staring intently at her computer with science books piled up around her.

"Oh, good! Then you won?"

"What?" Nicole finally pried her eyes away from the computer screen. She had to blink a few times to right her vision. "Oh no. No, we lost."

Her mom came in and sat down on the bed. "That's too bad! Was it close?"

"Mom, actually, would you mind if we talked later? I'm just trying to get some work done on my Science Fair project before tomorrow."

"But the fair isn't until Valentine's Day, before the dance, right?"

Nicole nodded. "I'm just trying to get a leg up.

You know I have a title to win, after all."

Mrs. Rissman smiled. "Ah, yes. You and that boy—what's his name again?"

Nicole rolled her eyes. "Jude," she reminded her mother.

"That's right! Jude Matthews. Such a smart boy. You two are always so competitive!"

"I have to beat him this year," Nicole said, her voice severe.

"Yes, well, it's good to try to be the best. And Dad and I admire your determination! But you know, sweetie, it's not whether you win or lose . . ."

". . . But how you play the game." Nicole finished

her mom's sentence. "I know. But I cannot let Jude Matthews beat me. I just can't."

"Just make sure the winning doesn't become more important than the learning, Nikki."

CHAPTER 5

Super Student!

STUDY THE EFFECTS OF DIFFERENT TYPES OF WATER ON AMPHIBIANS.

In Math class the next morning, last week's quizzes were handed back. Nicole was delighted to receive an A. Right below hers in the pile, she noted that Jamie Somers received a glaring red D.

In History, Nicole's diorama of the Egyptian pyramids towered over the rest of the class's projects. All except Jamie's, which was huge—but basically

just a pile of unidentifiable parts. "I'm sorry," he explained when he turned it in. "My dog ate my homework." The class tittered. "No, really!" he protested. "He did! We had to take him to the vet to get his stomach pumped."

"All right, class, take your seats." As the students filed into Science class, Mrs. Moss held up a clipboard. "I will pass around this sign-up sheet. Each pair should print their names and the project they'll be submitting for the Science Fair."

Around went the clipboard. Binah and Grace signed together. Amy and Charlotte paired up next. Charlotte handed the clipboard to Nicole, who neatly printed her name next to her project's description: "Study of the effects of different types of water on amphibians." She handed the clipboard to the student next to her.

"All right, class," Mrs. Moss said, taking the clipboard and scanning it quickly. "Wait. Nicole Rissman. You have not signed up with a partner."

"Oh, I know," replied Nicole. "I'm going to work by myself."

"Nicole," said Mrs. Moss sternly, "I'm afraid working in pairs was not a suggestion. It is a rule."

Nicole swallowed. Her heart pounded. "But—"

"Sorry I'm late!" The door to Mrs. Moss's classroom flew open, and Jamie Somers burst into the room. "It's not my fault, though! I just had to catch the end of the London versus Manchester hockey game. It was mad! They were tied the whole time, and then—"

"Perfect!" Mrs. Moss announced. "Jamie, please take your seat. You and Nicole will be partners for the Science Fair."

"All right!" Jamie beamed, flashing a thumbs-up at Nicole, who sat with her mouth open, shocked.

Partners with Jamie? Jamie Somers? No way.

"But, Mrs. Moss—" Nicole started, but her teacher nodded firmly at Nicole before she could finish her sentence.

"It's settled. Jamie, Nicole, good luck to you both."

And that as they say, was that!

CHAPTER 6

Nicole Tells It Like It Is (n't)

"You are soooo lucky!" Amy moaned. "Working with Jamie! I'm so jealous! No offense, Charlotte," she said to her actual Science Fair partner.

"None taken!" Charlotte whipped her pink scarf across her face to shield herself from the biting wind. "I'd work with him in a second! If you weren't available, of course," she said to Amy.

"Right." Amy smiled back.

"Are you kidding?" cried Nicole. "What am I going to do?!"

"Good question!" The girls gasped and turned to see Jamie coming down the front stairs. "But don't worry, Nicole. I've got a couple of ideas."

Nicole was less than eager to hear any ideas that came from Jamie Somers's decidedly unscientific head! "That's OK," she muttered. "I've already decided what I—I mean, we—are doing."

"OK, cool." Jamie bounded down the

stairs. "We'd better get started then, right?"

The English Roses nodded emphatically at Nicole, who stood there, mute. "We'll just leave you two to get to work," Amy said pointedly. "See you tomorrow, Nikki!" The Roses waved good-bye to Nicole, who stared after them imploringly. How could they leave her alone?

"Come on, don't look so serious," Jamie said, chucking Nicole on the shoulder.

"I am serious. About serious subjects. And Science is something I find serious. So unless you get serious, I think we're going to have a serious problem!"

Jamie stared at her for a moment, then broke into a grin. "Seriously?" he asked.

Nicole stuttered.

SERIOUSLY?

"I'm only kidding," Jamie said. "Look, let's go back inside. It's freezing out here!"

He wasn't even wearing a jacket. Nicole had to take pity on him. They headed back into school, Nicole wondering how things could possibly get any worse.

"OK, here's the deal," Nicole said, setting down her backpack on a chair in the empty cafeteria. She pulled out her notes and spread them across a table. "We're going to test the reaction of amphibious creatures to different types of water. We'll monitor their growth, behavior, energy level, weight patterns, and so on and so forth." She paused and pointed to a few charts and graphs she'd already started working on. "We'll chart our findings here, outline projected results here, and graph behavioral patterns here."

"Wow. You've really got this figured out," Jamie said, looking over her work. Nicole nodded.

"Yes. Well."

"Sooo . . . do I get a say?"

Nicole didn't know quite how to respond. She'd just assumed he would be happy to let her do all the work.

"Um, sure. I— Of course."

Jamie smiled again—a big, friendly smile that showed off perfect white teeth. "Thanks!" He stood up and started walking toward the back of the cafeteria.

"Um, where are you going?" Nicole called after him.

Jamie waved for her to follow him. "Well, I can't work on an empty stomach."

"I hate to break it to you, but the cafeteria is closed."

Jamie pulled a key chain out of his pocket and jangled the keys in the air. "Oh, really?" There was that smile again. It was hard not to smile back.

Not That Kind of a Date

"I can't believe Mrs. Appleby just gave you the keys!" Nicole looked around in wonder. They were in the middle of the cafeteria's pantry: a huge room stacked with treats, filling up every wall as far as the eye could see. Licorice vines, sour gummies, chocolate bars, chocolate balls, chocolate bricks . . . the delectable delights just went on and on.

"What can I say?" Jamie pulled a jar of Marshmallow Fluff off a high shelf. "Cafeteria ladies love me. Here . . . catch!" He tossed the jar at Nicole, who caught it perfectly. "Wish I always kicked as well as I threw just now." He sighed. "We really fell apart on the field the other night."

Nicole appreciated the look on his face. For once he looked actually . . . well, serious!

"Well . . ." Nicole searched for the right words. "You definitely played well. That goal was very impressive."

That seemed to do the trick; the smile was back. "Thanks. It was pretty exciting. Too bad it wasn't enough."

"You'll get them next time."

"We'd better. Losing is bad enough. But losing to Yorkshire?" Jamie made a face as he pulled down a loaf of white bread and some peanut butter. He scooped out a huge dollop of peanut butter and motioned to Nicole to add a layer of Marshmallow Fluff to the sandwiches taking form before him.

"That's how I feel about the Science Fair," Nicole confided as she spread the white froth on top. "There's this boy . . . Jude Matthews." She frowned, pausing mid-fluff-spread.

"I take it you're not a fan?" Jamie asked.

"That's putting it mildly. I just can't let him beat me. We have to win."

Jamie slapped on two pieces

THISH
ish
derishish!!!

of bread to top off the sandwiches. "That's the spirit!" He handed one sandwich to Nicole, then "clinked" his against hers. "Cheers! I'll eat to that!" He took a huge bite of the sandwich. Nicole smiled and did the same.

"YUM!" she exclaimed, her mouth full. "Thish ish derishish!"

"It's not rocket science, but it's pretty good, huh?"

Nicole nodded, and they both laughed.

As they finished their sandwiches and cleaned up the pantry, Jamie surprised Nicole with ideas and opinions that, she had to admit, would make their project much better than what she'd initially planned on her own.

"Huh," Nicole said, as Jamie locked the pantry door shut behind them.

"What?" he asked.

"Nothing. It's just . . . I'm just a little surprised. You didn't exactly seem like the bookworm type."

"What do you mean?" Jamie asked.

"Well . . . that diorama project. *The dog ate your homework?*"

"He did! Poor Seymore. He was puking up papier-mâché for a week."

"And what about the math quiz? A *D*?"

"You saw that?" Jamie looked embarrassed. "My little sister stuck the pages of my Math book together with gum, so I missed a whole chapter when I was studying."

"I'm—I'm sorry. I really misjudged you."

"No worries, Miss Rissman." Jamie shrugged. "I guess you had some pretty good reasons to do so."

"Well, if your sandwich-making skills are any indication, I think you're very talented!"

They opened the doors and entered the brisk winter twilight. The air was icy but refreshing. "Hey, let's meet again tomorrow," Jamie said, as they ran down the stairs.

"Ooh!" Nicole cried, almost careening right into a girl sitting at the foot of the steps. "I'm sorry, I didn't even see you there."

"That's OK," said Alexis Leeds. "You were . . ." She looked from Nicole to Jamie and back again. "You were a little busy."

"What are you doing here so late?" Nicole asked.

"Just finishing up a story for the newspaper," Alexis replied. "I might do well to ask you the same thing."

"Top-secret project!" Jamie chimed in. "Right, Nic?"

"Riiight." Nicole smiled back.

"Hmmmm," Alexis said, pulling out a spiral notebook from her back pocket.

Alexis Leeds watched the two new friends part ways. She smiled to herself, scribbling something furiously into her notebook.

CHAPTER 8

Valentine's Day Dance Dilemmas

Nicole could barely sleep that night. Visions of Science Fair projects and marshmallow sandwiches swirled in her head, and she woke up even before her alarm rang.

The walk to school seemed to take longer than usual. It didn't help that all her friends wanted to talk about was the Valentine's Day Dance.

"Who are you going with, Amy?" asked Charlotte.

"I don't know! I mean, Ryan is the cutest. But Max is so sweet. Or maybe Peter . . ."

"I wish I could ask Anthony, but with his football injury, I don't think he'll be up for dancing," Grace said. (Anthony Strong was an awesome footballer who was in Mr. Farburger's sixth-grade class.)

"I hope they have good music," Binah mused. "Papa's been helping me practice my dance moves."

"Ooh, good!" Charlotte clapped delightedly as they rounded the bend and approached the school building. "Nicole, who are you bringing?"

But before Nicole could answer, Jamie's voice rang out behind them.

"Hey, Nic! I had some thoughts last night. Want to meet real quick?"

Nicole glanced at her watch. Class started in ten

Ten MINUTES till class...

minutes. Typically, Nicole liked to be the first one in her seat, but this couldn't wait.

"Did you see that?" Amy exclaimed as Nicole and Jamie ran up the stairs.

"I can't believe she's not going straight to class," Binah remarked.

"What's come over her?" Charlotte asked.

"Is there something wrong with Nicole?" Alexis Leeds asked, appearing suddenly and taking the English Roses by surprise.

"No. She's fine," said Grace.

"What do you think is going on between her and Jamie?" Alexis probed.

"What? Nothing!" Grace exclaimed. "They're just partners for the Science Fair."

"Are you sure that's all they are?" Alexis asked, leaning in conspiratorially. "Because they sure looked cozy when I saw them together after school yesterday."

The English Roses exchanged looks. Alexis Leeds was well known to be the biggest gossip at Hampstead.

"Yes, we're sure," Charlotte said stiffly. "Come on, girls," she said to her friends. "Excuse us, Alexis. We have to get to class."

"Nicole doesn't seem too worried about that," Alexis pointed out. The English Roses couldn't exactly argue, but they weren't about to give Alexis any ammunition.

Brrrriiiiing!

Nicole and Jamie ran into the classroom just as the last notes of the bell faded away. *Phew!* thought

Nicole. *That was close.* But it had been worth it—Jamie was turning out to be a fabulous partner. She couldn't have been more wrong about him!

Just as she smiled to herself about the delightful turn of events in the Science Fair partner category, her thoughts were interrupted by a whisper.

"Cutting it a little close, aren't we? What about your perfect attendance record?"

Nicole turned around to face Alexis, who sat behind her. "It's still intact," she whispered back.

"Ladies," Mrs. Moss chastised from the front of the room. "Class is starting."

"I'm sorry, Mrs. Moss. It won't happen again," Nicole apologized. She turned around quickly, not noticing the small journalist's notebook Alexis began to scribble into as soon as Nicole turned toward the front of the class.

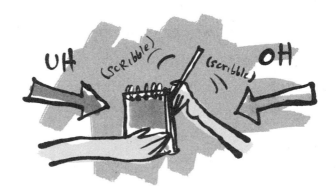

A picture-perfect Valentine's Day Dance

CHAPTER 9

Operation Get Gorgeous

The next few days sped by in a blur. All of Hampstead seemed to have contracted Valentine's fever. Amy's room was filled with sky-high piles of fashion magazines; she'd picked all her favorite looks to help inspire her (and her friends') dress choices for the dance.

Binah and her father had mastered the waltz, the box step, and the fox-trot. She practiced extra hard, knowing that her dad would actually be at the dance to see her moves in person. Binah had mentioned to Mr. Rossi that Miss Fluffernutter was to be one of the chaperones at the dance; and the very next day, he announced that he too would be there to supervise!

Charlotte was working on a color palette and different hairstyle options that would best reflect each Rose's style and personality.

Even Grace, the tomboy of the group, was getting into the girly-girl fun of it all. It was kind of like getting ready for a big game—exciting and scary, all at the same time!

Only Nicole had other things on her mind. She and Jamie met after school every day, even getting together on weekends to work on their Science Fair project. It was definitely a unique experience for her. Nicole loved her friends, but she'd always preferred doing schoolwork alone. This time, though, things were different. Nicole realized that Jamie had talents in different areas from her own. She was organized; Jamie was creative. She was diligent and detail oriented; Jamie was a spontaneous and abstract thinker. By putting their different skills together, they became a more powerful force. One that, she

hoped, would soon be kicking Jude's butt!

"OK, girls, we're down to the wire. It's time to get cracking." Amy held court on the front steps after school one day, her friends gathered around to hear her important speech. "The dance is next Friday—just one week from today! And we still don't have our outfits down to a science!"

Charlotte nodded. "The car will be here in . . ."— she checked her watch—"five minutes. Operation Get Gorgeous for the Valentine's Day Dance is now officially in effect!"

Binah and Grace squealed with delight. But one of the Roses was suspiciously quiet.

"All right, Nikki. What's up?" Grace inquired.

"Nothing. It's just—you guys go ahead. I don't need a new dress."

Charlotte gasped. "You absolutely *do* need a new dress for the dance!"

"This is not even up for discussion!" Amy put her foot down. "Nicole, you have been entirely too obsessed with this Science Fair project. I know it's important to you, but we barely ever get to see you anymore!"

"We miss you," Binah agreed.

"It's not fair that Jamie's the only one who gets to hang out with you," Grace added.

"Yeah! He can spare you for one afternoon," Charlotte proclaimed.

Nicole looked around at her friends' faces. She

hadn't meant to neglect them. *I guess I can take one day off*, she thought. She smiled. "OK, OK! I'm in."

"Yay!" the English Roses cried delightedly.

"Jamie will definitely forgive you for missing a study session when he sees how gorgeous you'll look at the dance," Amy exclaimed. Nicole rolled her eyes but smiled as the girls climbed into the sleek black limousine that pulled up at that very moment.

Alexis Leeds looked on as the limo pulled away. "Excuse me," she said to a group of passing students, who stopped to see what she wanted. "Can I borrow a pen? I think I have come up with the perfect headline for this week's front page."

CHAPTER 10

A No-Science Zone

It felt like snow. The air was bright and cold, the kind that cools your lungs and freezes your breath in crystallized puffs. Nicole breathed deep as she headed toward the warm, glowing dress boutique, her face tilted up at the gray sky. Her friends were right; she needed a break from her hard work.

Charlotte's dress

"Ooh! This, this is the one!" Charlotte cried, holding up a stunning cocktail-length dress with a bold purple and black striped pattern.

"It's fabulous," Amy agreed, smiling. She sighed. "There had better be some cute Yorkshire boys at this dance! At least one prince out of all the frogs."

"Speaking of frogs," Nicole piped up, "did I tell you Jamie's latest idea for our project? Instead of one frog in each aquarium, we're putting in two—"

"Ding ding ding!" Charlotte interrupted. "Sorry, Nikki, but this is a no-science zone. Only girl-talk allowed!"

Nicole smiled. "All right, fine. What do you want to talk about?"

"How about . . ." Charlotte smiled mischievously. "You and Jamie!"

"What about me and Jamie?" Nicole asked.

"Has he asked you yet?" Amy jumped in.

"Asked me what?" Nicole was confused.

"To the dance, of course!" Grace laughed.

Nicole frowned. "I don't know what you're—"

Binah smiled encouragingly. "You and Jamie are going to the dance together, right?"

"Wrong!" Nicole cried. "Where did you get that crazy idea?"

"Oh!" Binah apologized. "We just thought . . . You seem to be getting along so well, and spending so much time—"

"We're partners!" Nicole exclaimed. "We've been working on our project, not planning dates. Honestly, I haven't even thought about the dance for a second until today. I have to focus all my energy on the fair if I'm going to beat Jude Matthews. Valentine's Day just isn't on my radar screen."

"Are you sure it's not on Jamie's?" Grace asked.

"Positive," Nicole nodded.

"If you say so . . ." Charlotte singsonged.

"I say so!" Nicole said firmly. "Now, Amy, hand me something frilly already and let's change the subject."

Amy laughed, and the other girls joined in.

The rest of the afternoon was filled with fun, fashion, sweets, shopping, and other assorted "girl-stuff." Nicole dutifully avoided the topic of the Science Fair and soon got swept up in the delights of the day: new fruit-flavored lip gloss at the cosmetics counter; Oreo milk shakes at the Soda Shoppe; Charlotte treating everyone to manicures at the salon. It was, all in all, a very lovely day indeed.

amy's
dress

Binah's
dress

gracie's
dress

CHAPTER 11

A Miserable Monday

ome on, come on . . . Nicole tapped her boot anxiously and glanced at her watch for about the zillionth time. Heaps of bright, fluffy snow were piled high on both sides of the driveway, and an icy white slick covered the road. She did not want to be late today! She and Jamie hadn't been able to get together because of the weather, and now she had so many new ideas she wanted to discuss with him! The Science Fair was this Friday!

The ride to school seemed to take forever. She tried to encourage Charlotte's driver to speed up, but the slippery roads made driving hazardous, and everyone was traveling well below the speed limit. They got to Hampstead only a few minutes before the bell.

Bursting into the classroom, she searched for Jamie's mop of blond hair in the crowd of students peeling off their warm winter wear.

"Oh, he's not here yet," said Emily Stanford.

"Who?" Nicole asked, confused.

"Jamie, of course," Emily replied.

"How'd you—" But before Nicole could finish

her sentence, something stopped her in her tracks. The front page of the *Hampstead Hornblower* stared up at her from a nearby desk. The boldfaced headline blared: HAMPSTEAD HOT COUPLE ALERT: JAMIE SOMERS AND NICOLE RISSMAN, A PERFECT PAIR!

The bell was ringing, but she couldn't move her feet. She just stood there, staring at those words, unable to speak.

"Hey, Nic!" She heard his voice but couldn't turn to face him. Jamie nudged her. "*Phew!* Just made it. Didn't want to be late today— I've got a ton to talk to you about! Let's meet right after school, OK?"

Mrs. Moss cleared her throat from the front of the room, signaling the start of class. Nicole blinked; it was as if the room was filled with a hazy fog. She turned away from Jamie without answering and managed to find her seat. Behind her, Alexis Leeds tapped her on the shoulder.

"Looks like you made big news!" she whispered to Nicole. "Must feel good to land both the man and the front page!" Nicole sank into her seat, willing the day to be over already. This was officially the worst Monday of her life.

CHAPTER 12

It's Just Gossip, Girl

Have you ever had one of those moments when you're convinced you are the focus of everyone's attention? When every time you hear people laugh, you're just sure they're laughing at you? When it seems the whole world is in on the joke except for one person—you?

Well, Nicole was having one of those moments.

As soon as class ended, she was out the door and halfway down the hall before her friends could catch up with her. Laughter rang in her ears. Whispers prickled her skin like fingernails on a chalkboard. She felt as if she was going to scream.

"Hey! Nic! Where's the fire?"

Nicole squeezed her eyes shut. No, no, no . . . she had to get away. She could feel a thousand eyes on her, all watching to see what "Hampstead's Hot Couple" would do next.

"So, do you want to come over after school?

We've only got 'til Friday! I wanted to talk to you about—"

But Nicole couldn't take it anymore. She felt as if a glaring spotlight was trained right on them; she longed to be back hiding in the shadowy background. This situation was her worst nightmare!

"I'm sorry. I— " Nicole looked away, avoiding Jamie's worried eyes. "I have to go." And she bolted, leaving Jamie staring after her in confusion. A few moments later, the rest of the Roses caught up to him in the hallway.

"Was that Nicole?" Grace asked.

Jamie nodded. "She seemed really odd just now. Just . . . ran off. No explanation. Is everything all right?"

The girls exchanged a concerned glance. Charlotte looked down at the newspaper in her hands. Everything was definitely not all right.

"Come on, Nikki. It's not a big deal!" Grace stood outside a locked bathroom stall, calling through the door to Nicole, who was hiding out inside. "No one thinks anything of it."

"It's idle gossip!" Binah agreed.

"Everyone knows that Alexis will say anything to get people reading her paper," Amy chimed in.

"People will forget about it by tomorrow!" Charlotte cried.

Nicole shook her head. They didn't understand. How could she face anyone after this? How could she face Jamie? Did he think she liked him? How would he ever take her seriously now? How would anyone? A tear rolled down her cheek.

"Oh, Nikki, no!" Binah cried, hearing Nicole sniffling from the other side of the door.

"I'm fine," Nicole's muffled voice responded. "Please, I don't— I just want to be alone."

"We love you, Nikki," Amy said quietly. The girls nodded. Nicole sniffled in response. And one

by one, the Roses left their friend in the bathroom to "be alone."

"She'll come around," said Charlotte hopefully.

"All we can do is support her," Binah said.

The rest of the Roses agreed. "The fair is this Friday," Grace reminded them. "That's too important for her to let some rumor ruin all her hard work. I'm sure of it."

The truth was, none of them felt particularly "sure" about anything just then. But sometimes telling yourself something can help you believe it. And at that moment, the English Roses told themselves Nicole would soon be just fine.

CHAPTER 13

Everything Hurts

ut Nicole was not fine. In fact, she was so un-fine that the next morning she turned off her alarm clock and hid under the covers.

"Nikki? Honey, are you all right?" her mother asked, peeking into Nicole's room and finding her daughter huddled under her comforter in a sad little heap.

Nicole shook her head. Her throat felt dry and her eyes burned. Of course, that might have been because she'd cried herself to sleep the night before.

"I feel positively awful," she croaked. Her mother rushed over, concerned.

"Hmm. You don't feel as if you have a temperature," Mrs. Rissman murmured, pressing her palm against Nicole's forehead.

"I feel hot," Nicole objected. "And my throat hurts. Everything hurts," she moaned, flinging herself back onto her bed. "I don't think I can go to school today."

Her mother was shocked. "Well, you must be ill if you can't go to school! You've never wanted to miss a day in your life! Even when you had the chicken pox, you hid your spots under a turtleneck sweater, hoping I wouldn't notice! And if it hadn't been the middle of July, I might not have thought anything of it." Mrs. Rissman smiled at the memory. But Nicole was not amused.

"Do you need to see a doctor?" Mrs. Rissman asked. "I'm worried . . ."

"Don't be." Nicole shook her head. "I'll be fine. I just need rest. And quiet," she added.

"All right, then. I'll leave you be. Get some sleep, dear." She kissed her daughter on the top of her head and pulled the covers up to her chin. "I'll be in to check on you in a bit."

"Can you shut the door behind you?" Nicole asked, already feeling the tears pricking behind her eyes. Her mother was hardly out of the room before they spilled over, dampening Nicole's pillow.

Nicole stayed in bed all of Tuesday, and the next day too. The English Roses called her about a zillion times (at least it seemed so to them!), but Nicole told her mom she was too sick to talk.

Of course, Jamie was calling, too. The Science Fair was just days away, and the two of them had a project to finish! But Nicole refused to take his calls. She would have felt bad about leaving him in

Nicole –
Jamie called
♡ mom

the lurch if she allowed herself to think about him at all. It was easier just to hide and try to keep her mind blank.

On Thursday afternoon, the doorbell rang. Nicole heard voices downstairs but pulled the covers over her head. Whoever it was, she didn't care. That is, until she heard her bedroom door open.

"Mom, I told you; I don't want to see anyone," she called out from underneath the covers.

"Well, I want to see you," a voice retorted. A voice that did not belong to her mother. Nicole cringed. Uh-oh . . .

"Look, I don't know what's wrong with you," Jamie continued from the doorway. He sounded worried, and a little bit sad. "But you're always the one talking about what it means to be 'serious.' You take your work seriously; you take your friends seriously; and until now, I thought you were taking me seriously." He paused. "I guess . . . I guess I was wrong." He paused again, as if waiting for her to respond. But she just couldn't. Finally, Jamie spoke again. "OK. I guess that's it. I just wanted to say that. Feel better, Nicole."

And with that he was gone.

CHAPTER 14

The Power of Words

Friday! Fridays are, as you probably know, the opposite of Mondays. Mondays are boring; Fridays are brilliant. Mondays are long and dreary; Fridays fly by in a flash! And this Friday was particularly important.

"What? Still?" cried Charlotte, her pink cell phone pressed to her ear. "Really?"

"What? Tell us!" the Roses clamored.

Charlotte covered the receiver with her palm and whispered, "Mrs. Rissman says Nikki's still sick. She's not coming to school today!"

"OK. Thanks. No, we understand," Charlotte continued into her phone. "Please tell her we say feel better." She snapped her phone shut, then turned to her friends. "Girls, this has gone on long enough. Something has to be done."

Meanwhile, Nicole was—you guessed it—huddled under her covers. She peeked at her bedside clock and sighed. Her friends would be in Science

class right now. *Perfect,* thought Nicole. *Just perfect.*

The seconds, minutes, and hours ticked by. Nicole lay in bed, trying not to think about what day it was. But no matter how hard she tried, she couldn't *not* remember that today was Friday, February 14.

The day of the Science Fair.

She felt truly awful. Worse than ever, actually. She willed herself not to think about Jamie, forced to present their project all alone. She tried not to think about Jude, smugly winning the fair again. She tried not to think about her friends, getting ready for the Valentine's Day Dance without her. She hated lying here alone, but she couldn't figure out how to get up. It was as if she was trapped. Trapped in a jail she'd built herself!

"Nikki? Are you up?"

"Yeah." Nicole sighed.

Mrs. Rissman came in, holding a large box tied with a bright green ribbon. Nicole sat up, intrigued. "This came for you," her mother said, setting the box down on the bed. Nicole eyed the package. But before she could open it, her mother continued. "Nikki, your father and I love you so much. We're proud of you no matter what." She paused and looked her daughter in the eye. "But you need to make sure you're always proud of your-

self. Even when things get hard, you need to make sure you're being the best Nicole you can be. Think about that. OK?"

Nicole nodded. Her mother smiled lovingly. "OK." Then she turned and left her daughter alone with the mysterious gift.

Nicole pulled the end of the satin ribbon and untied the bow. Slowly, she lifted the lid of the box.

The first thing she saw was the newspaper. A handwritten note was attached to the front page with a paper clip. Nicole pulled it free and began to read:

Dear Nicole,

A true journalist prides herself on honesty and accuracy. A true journalist would never publish rumors or gossip.

I've decided to be a true journalist.

I know you haven't been feeling well lately; I hope this helps.

Best,

Alexis Leeds

Nicole lifted the newspaper. One article took up the front page:

A PERFECT PAIR: CAN HAMPSTEAD BEAT YORKSHIRE AT THE FAIR?

The annual Science Fair is approaching, and Hampstead has only one hope of winning: the dream team of Jamie Somers and Nicole Rissman. These two science superstars are out to prove that two heads are better than one. Can Rissman and Somers unveil a project that will put Yorkshire to shame? Recently, rumors that the two were in a romantic relationship were proven to be false. Let's hope these friends and partners can bring home first prize for Hampstead!

Shocked, Nicole stared at the article for a moment before she realized the box still wasn't empty. She reached inside and took out another note:

Nikki,
We love you. Hampstead
needs you. Jamie needs you.
And we need you.
Love,
The English Roses

Nicole held the note to her chest, flushed with pride and love for her wonderful, incredible friends. It's an amazing thing to have people in your life who know what you need better than you know yourself. She smiled and leaped out of bed. Suddenly, she was feeling *much* better!

CHAPTER 15

The Froggy Fracas

"Very nice, Mr. Matthews. Very impressive indeed." The Science Fair was in full swing as the judges stood in front of Jude's project, admiring his efforts. He smiled as they marked his scores on their clipboards.

As the judges walked out of the room for a break, Jude caught Amy's eye. "Have you heard from Nicole?" he asked when she came over.

Amy shook her head sadly. "No. We haven't heard a peep from her."

Jude looked dejected. "That's too bad. I was really looking forward to seeing what she came up with. She always has the most interesting ideas."

Suddenly, a huge gasp and a shriek came from the other side of the room!

"Oh no!" Amy cried when she saw what was happening. Jamie Somers was in crisis. The Roses ran over.

"Uh, hello!" Jamie welcomed them as they approached his project. Don't worry; I have things under control. . . ."

But "under control" was the exact opposite of how Jamie had things. For his (and, for that matter, Nicole's) scientific masterpiece had devolved into

a mass of slippery, slimy, hopping baby frogs!

"Aaah! Get them off! Get them off me!" Charlotte shrieked, leaping onto a nearby chair to escape the overly active amphibians. Frogs were everywhere. Little green specks bounced all over the floor, on tables, even into other people's projects! Jamie struggled to contain them, but it was no use.

"Sorry, so sorry," he stuttered, grabbing at the chaos-creating culprits. "Oh, crazy. Let me just—ooh, there's one in your . . . " He reached up and plucked a baby frog out of Amy's hair. She let out an ear-piercing scream, scattering a cluster of frogs far and wide. The entire room erupted into shrieking, screaming, scampering mayhem. Jamie slumped into a chair, his head in his hands. "The judges will be back any second!" he moaned.

This is what a blood-curdling scream looks like →

(grace loves snapping)

Suddenly, Grace was in the middle of the scene, taking charge of the froggy fracas. "Okay, people, let's get this under control. Worthington! Hudson! Somers!" She snapped her fingers, and the boys stood at attention. "Spread out to all corners! Help me scoop up these rascals and put them back in their tanks." She turned to the other Roses. "You girls get outside and stall those judges. Do whatever it takes!"

The class sprang into action at Grace's

command. Soon the amphibians were all in their respective tanks, croaking happily.

Jamie ran over to Grace. "Whew! You're a life-saver, Harrison. Thanks!"

"No problem," Grace replied. "Consider it thanks for the times you've rescued the Hampstead footballers with your superstar kicks."

The crowd finally quieted down as the froggy fracas subsided.

"Ladies and gentlemen!" A voice echoed. Everyone looked up to see Nicole standing at the front of the room with the judges fanned out behind her.

"Our project is based on the effects of different kinds of water on amphibious creatures," Nicole stated.

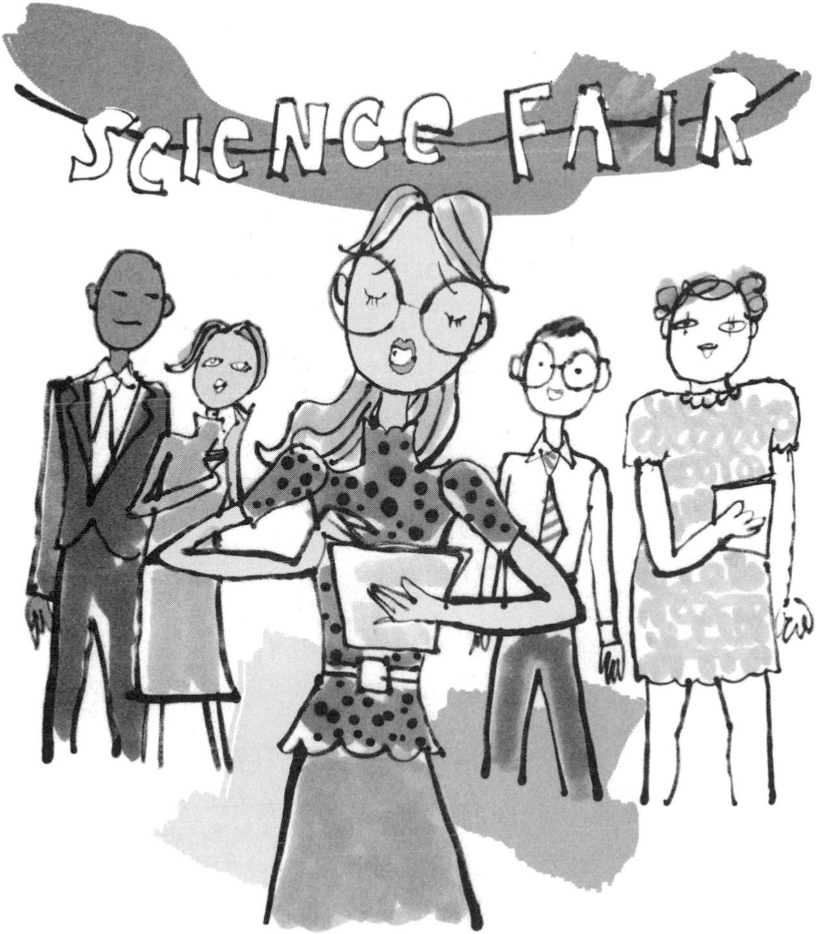
SCIENCE FAIR

"As you can see, in aquarium number 1, the frogs living in swamp water reached the top percentile in height and weight," Nicole continued, as she made her way through the room toward Jamie and their project. "The frogs in tap water, as you see in aquarium number 2, were a step behind. They're a little underweight for the average, but still perfectly healthy." She arrived next to Jamie and stopped, pointing to the third tank populated with bouncing baby frogs. "But the frogs in mineral water . . . Here's where things got interesting! As you can see, our two sample frogs produced a number of babies far greater than that of the average amphibious parent." The frogs seemed to jump even higher, as if to emphasize her point. "Obviously, the minerals in the water had a profound effect on frog fertility. And, I might add, if my brilliant partner hadn't suggested putting two frogs in each tank, we would never have come up with this incredible evidence!" She smiled at Jamie, who perked up.

"So, if you'll take the time to read our data, I think you'll be impressed with some rather amazing findings," Nicole suggested, handing a stack of

charts and graphs to the judges. As they conferred over the paperwork, Nicole met Jamie's eyes. "I'm so sorry," she mouthed to him. Jamie beamed back at her, and she had the sudden feeling that everything was going to be OK.

CHAPTER 16

Toad-ally Amazing

"Nic, you saved my life!" Jamie threw an arm around Nicole as they exited the room. The fair was over, and everyone else was already at the Valentine's Day Dance. Jamie and Nicole had stayed behind to return their frogs safely to Mrs. Moss's classroom.

"Are you kidding?" Nicole exclaimed. "I practically ruined your life! I can't believe those frogs escaped during the fair!"

"I know. It was toad-ally amazing!" Jamie said. Nicole burst into laughter. "There. That's what I like to see." Jamie smiled. "Serious Nicole not taking things too seriously."

"I think I've learned my lesson where that's concerned," Nicole replied. "I'm really sorry, Jamie. About everything."

"Nothing to be sorry for," Jamie said back. And Nicole could tell he meant it. "So!" He ran a hand through his blond hair. "What do you say we hit that dance everyone's been so excited about? I brought my suit and everything."

Nicole looked down at her stained skirt and

water-soaked sweater. Cleaning up after those frogs had been a dirty job! She shook her head. "I don't think so. I'm not exactly dressed for it."

"Aw, come on," Jamie coaxed. "They're naming the Science Fair winner at the dance! You can't miss that."

"Yes, well, you can fill me in later. Besides"—Nicole grinned —"winning isn't everything."

"Are you kidding?" Jamie gasped. "Who are you, and what have you done with Nicole?"

"I told you I've changed!" she laughed.

"Well then," came a voice from behind her, "you can change again . . . into this!"

Nicole spun around just in time to catch the silky yellow gown that floated into her arms. She looked up. There were Binah, Charlotte, Grace, and Amy, all dressed up and smiling back at her.

"Go ahead," Amy directed. "Put it on. We've got a Valentine's Day Dance to attend!"

The cafeteria had been transformed into a winter wonderland. White sparkling "snowdrifts"

lined the room. Crystal snowflakes danced, dangling from the ceiling. The tables were covered with cloths of red, white, and pink. Rose petals dusted the dance floor.

"Oh!" Binah breathed. "It's beautiful!" The other girls nodded, mesmerized. It truly looked like a dream.

Just then Mrs. Moss turned on a microphone and cleared her throat.

"Ahem. Excuse me. It's now time to announce the winner of the annual Science Fair." Students murmured excitedly. Jamie ran over and stood beside Nicole.

"Hey," he whispered. "Even if we don't win, I'd work with you again in a heartbeat!"

"Same here!" Nicole whispered back, smiling.

Today was turning out to be the perfect day! Their project was perfect and so was her dress. Her friends had chosen just the right style for her— pretty but not too frilly. And it fit as if it was made for her! Silver sandals with emerald clasps completed the look.

And even Nicole had to admit that Jamie looked smashing in a dark blue suit and green striped tie. In fact, Nicole could see about fifty girls eying him shyly from all over the room.

"And this year's winner of the Science Fair is . . ." A hush fell over the crowd. Nicole's heart pounded in her chest. Jamie wasn't even breathing, he was so nervous. She could feel her friends behind her, waiting anxiously.

" . . . Jamie Somers and Nicole Rissman!" The

room erupted in wild cheers, and Jamie swept Nicole up into a huge hug.

"We did it!"

"We certainly did!" Nicole laughed, hugging him back. She couldn't believe she had been so silly as to almost miss this moment!

"Excuse me," a voice suddenly piped in. Nicole turned. "I didn't mean to interrupt. . . ."

"No, that's OK." Nicole smoothed her skirt as she looked up and met Jude Matthews's brown eyes.

"I just wanted to say . . . Congratulations, Nicole."

"Thanks, Jude. That means a lot."

"It was quite a project!"

"That it was!" Nicole smiled. "And yours looked really interesting, too."

Just then the music shifted to a slow song. "Swaying room as the music starts . . ." it began.

"So," Jude said. "I was wondering . . ." He paused, nervous, and took a breath. "Do you . . . do you want to dance?"

Did she want to dance? With Jude? Nicole looked around. On one side of the room, all of

Hampstead seemed to be staring at her; on the other, Yorkshire was watching, too. Did she want to dance? She felt herself blushing, all eyes on her. Did she want to dance?

And then she realized: She did!

"Absolutely," Nicole said. Jude's face lit up. "I'd like that very much." And without another thought, she took his hand and led him to the center of the dance floor.

"What I'm dying to say . . ." the lyrics belted, "is that I'm crazy for you. . . ." As Nicole and Jude took to the floor, the rest of the students began to pair up. Even Miss Fluffernutter joined in . . . and no one was happier to see her dance

partner than Binah, who smiled to see her father leading her favorite teacher in a picture-perfect waltz. Miss Fluffernutter's dress was even fluffier than her hair (can you imagine?!), but Mr. Rossi maneuvered around it like a pro. He winked at his daughter as he twirled past, dipping Miss Fluffernutter so deep that her hairdo practically touched the floor!

Suddenly, the music changed and the jiggy beat of an up-tempo tune filled the air. "All right!" The English Roses grinned at one another. "The hip-hop bus stop!" It was a dance they had perfected during one of their many sleepover parties the year

before. The girls began to move their heads back and forth and stomp their feet rhythmically on the floor until a crowd formed around them.

One by one, the others joined the Roses in their dance until the dance floor was a whirlwind of flying arms and stamping feet and sweaty, smiling faces. The division between Hampstead and Yorkshire was no more! The two schools became one, the music soared, and the sparkling snowflakes swirled over

the students spinning in a whirling, twirling, happy Valentine's Day Dance.

The End

PREVIOUS BOOKS BY MADONNA

PICTURE BOOKS:

The English Roses
Mr. Peabody's Apples
Yakov and the Seven Thieves
The Adventures of Abdi
Lotsa de Casha
The English Roses: Too Good To Be True

CHAPTER BOOKS:

Friends for Life!
Good-Bye, Grace?
The New Girl
A Rose by Any Other Name
Big-Sister Blues
Being Binah
Hooray for the Holidays!

COMING SOON:

Runway Rose

MADONNA RITCHIE was born in Bay City, Michigan, and now lives in London and Los Angeles with her husband, movie director Guy Ritchie, and her children, Lola, Rocco, and David. She has recorded 18 albums and appeared in 18 movies. This is the eighth in her series of chapter books. She has also written six picture books for children, starting with the international bestseller *The English Roses*, which was released in 40 languages and more than 100 countries.

JEFFREY FULVIMARI was born in Akron, Ohio. He started coloring when he was two, and has never stopped. Soon after graduating from The Cooper Union in New York City, he began drawing for magazines and television commercials around the globe. He currently lives in a log cabin in upstate New York, and is happiest when surrounded by stacks of paper and magic markers.